Kitty's Magic

Ruby the Runaway Kitten

The Kitty's Magic series

Misty the Scared Kitten

Shadow the Lonely Cat

Ruby the Runaway Kitten

Star the Little Farm Cat

Coming soon

Frost and Snowdrop the Stray Kittens

Sooty the Birthday Cat

Kitty's magic

Ruby the Runaway Kitten

Ella Moonheart

illustrated by Dave Williams

BLOOMSBURY
CHILDREN'S BOOKS
NEW YORK   LONDON   OXFORD   NEW DELHI   SYDNEY

BLOOMSBURY CHILDREN'S BOOKS
Bloomsbury Publishing Inc., part of Bloomsbury Publishing Plc
1385 Broadway, New York, NY 10018

First published in Great Britain in February 2017 by Bloomsbury Publishing Plc
Published in the United States of America in June 2018 by Bloomsbury Children's Books
www.bloomsbury.com

Bloomsbury books may be purchased for business or promotional use. For information on bulk
purchases please contact Macmillan Corporate and Premium Sales Department at
specialmarkets@macmillan.com

Library of Congress Cataloging-in-Publication Data
available upon request
ISBN 978-1-68119-389-2 (paperback) • ISBN 978-1-68119-702-9 (hardcover)
ISBN 978-1-68119-390-8 (e-book)

Typeset by RefineCatch Limited, Bungay, Suffolk
Printed and bound in the U.S.A. by Berryville Graphics Inc., Berryville, Virginia
2 4 6 8 10 9 7 5 3   (paperback)
2 4 6 8 10 9 7 5 3 1   (hardcover)

To find out more about our authors and books visit www.bloomsbury.com and
sign up for our newsletters.

Kitty's Magic

Ruby the Runaway Kitten

Chapter 1

"Yes! I'm nearly at the end of level three!" said Kitty Kimura excitedly, pressing the buttons on her game controller. "I just have to jump over this puddle, tiptoe past the dog kennel, and I'm almost home."

"Go on, Kitty!" cried her best friend, Jenny. "I love this part of the game."

"Me too," added their friend Evie. "You're so good at it, Kitty!"

It was spring break, and Kitty and Jenny had been invited to Evie's house for the afternoon. They had made up a dance routine in the backyard, then tried out Evie's glittery felt-tips, all the while playing with Evie's gorgeous new kitten, Ruby. Ruby was only a couple of months old, and she was a very special breed of cat called a Bengal. This meant that her fur was almost golden, with dark spots that made her look like a tiny, adorable leopard. Now the girls were playing an exciting new game called Catventure on Evie's games console, taking turns playing the game and fussing over the kitten.

"How many of your nine lives have you used up, Kitty?" joked Evie.

Kitty giggled as she finished the level and handed her controller over to Jenny. She was eager to get back to playing with Ruby. She bent down to tickle Ruby's soft tummy, grinning as the kitten rolled around happily on the carpet. Evie grabbed the fishing-rod cat toy that they'd been playing with and dangled it over Ruby, who swatted playfully at the little stuffed fish on the end of the line.

But Evie frowned as a high-pitched wail broke out, which they could easily hear even over the noise of the computer game. "Dad!" she yelled. "He's crying again!"

Evie's baby brother, Joe, was strapped

into his bouncy chair near the television. He was just three months old, with big brown eyes and lovely chubby cheeks. Kitty thought he was so sweet. He had been napping when the girls came in, but the music from their game must have woken him up, and now he was crying noisily.

"Come on then, young man!" said Evie's dad cheerfully as he breezed in, unbuckling the straps on the bouncy chair and gently picking Joe up. "Let's go wander around the backyard, shall we, so we don't disturb your big sister and her friends?"

As her dad stepped outside, Evie sighed. "Joe cried for hours last night too," she explained to Kitty and Jenny.

"Mom and Dad and I were all watching a movie together, but we kept having to pause it. In the end it got too late and I had to go to bed without watching the ending. Dad even said he'd make us some popcorn, but he didn't have time. Baby brothers are cute, but they can be so annoying!"

"Definitely!" agreed Jenny, grinning. "Although Barney's a lot of fun, now that he's a bit older."

Kitty smiled. She was an only child, but she'd always wanted a little brother or sister, so secretly she thought Evie was really lucky. Baby Joe *did* need lots of attention, though!

Ding-dong! The doorbell rang, and Kitty heard Evie's mom go answer it.

"Hello, Mrs. Kimura! Come on in. Kitty's just with the girls in the living room."

"Hi, Grandma!" called Kitty. She gave little Ruby one last tickle and then ran into the hall to give her grandmother a hug. Grandma lived with Kitty and her parents, so Kitty and Grandma were very close. Grandma was from Japan, and she had the same dark eyes and straight, shiny black hair as Kitty— though Grandma's bob had a streak of pure white running through it.

"Hello, my darling," said Grandma. "Have you had a nice afternoon? Mom and Dad are staying late at the shop tonight, so it's going to be just the two of us."

Kitty's parents owned a little shop on Willow Street, just around the corner from their house, which sold all sorts of special Japanese trinkets and objects. They often had to work late or take business trips to Japan, but Kitty didn't mind—it meant she could spend more time with her grandma.

Kitty said goodbye to Jenny and Evie and thanked Evie's mom for having her. She peeped out of the kitchen window and waved goodbye to Evie's dad, who was still strolling round the garden with baby Joe nestled in his arms, now fast asleep. Then she and Grandma began to walk home.

"It's such a lovely day. Let's go home through the park, shall we?" suggested Grandma. "I don't know about you, but I'd like to ride on the swings!"

The park was busy with children playing soccer, swinging on the swings, and feeding the ducks at the edge of the park's small pond. Grandma nodded toward a quiet shaded area underneath a row of oak trees nearby. Three cats

were playing in the grass, pouncing on each other and tumbling around. Kitty realized that one of them, a small silver tabby, was Jenny's cat, Misty.

Grandma winked at Kitty. "If you're careful, you can go and play with the cats for a little while before dinner," she whispered.

Kitty looked at Grandma's mysterious expression, then grinned. She understood exactly what Grandma meant. Kitty had a very special secret, and Grandma was the only other person in the world who knew it!

For her whole life, Kitty had loved cats, but she had always thought she was allergic to them. Her nose itched, twitched, and tickled whenever she was anywhere near a cat. Then one day, Grandma had given Kitty a gift: a pretty silver necklace with some strange words engraved on it. That night, Kitty had stayed over at Jenny's house, and she'd had a sneezing fit that she'd thought was because of Misty, Jenny's cat. But to her amazement, something magical had happened. Kitty had turned into a cat!

Grandma had explained to Kitty that her amazing ability had been passed down through the family for years and years. She said that the special necklace's words would help Kitty to change back and forth from human to cat whenever she wanted to. Kitty thought she was the luckiest girl in the world. And over time, she had been getting better at using her magical power. She loved padding around her town after dark in her cat form, when all her human friends were tucked up in bed. She especially loved making friends with the other cats she met, including her very best cat friend, Misty. But Kitty had to be very careful not to let any other humans find out about her special gift. If they did, Grandma had explained that the magic would be lost forever.

Kitty glanced around to make sure that no one in the park was watching. She stepped behind a bush and reached for her necklace. Kitty took a deep breath. Then, very quietly, she muttered the mysterious words on the pendant.

"Human hands to kitten paws,
Human fingers, kitten claws."

As a warm, tingling feeling swept through her fingers and toes, Kitty closed her eyes. Her legs, arms, and belly fizzed as though they were full of thousands of tiny lemonade bubbles. It felt like she was being tickled all over her body.

When the feeling stopped, Kitty opened her eyes. The first thing she noticed was that she could see every tiny detail on the bush in front of her: the pattern on the leaves, the droplets of rain from earlier that day, and even a row of ants scuttling along. She glanced down and instead of her hands she saw two small white, furry paws, with neat little claws, at the end of fuzzy black legs. Her silver necklace had been replaced by a pretty collar with a tiny picture of a girl engraved on it. Kitty was a cat!

Chapter 2

Kitty trotted out from behind the bush and ran to join the cats playing under the oak trees. She loved the feeling of the grass beneath her paws and the swish of her tail behind her. When Misty caught sight of Kitty, the little silver tabby let out a happy meow.

"Hi, Kitty! I was hoping you'd come out to play today!"

Kitty bumped heads gently with Misty to say hello. She knew the other cats too: a friendly, fluffy gray named Smoky, and an excited young tortoiseshell called Bella. They all purred a greeting, and another cat appeared by Kitty's side: a small black cat with a patch of pure white fur by one of her ears.

"Suki!" said Bella.

Kitty purred happily. "Hi, Grandma," she meowed, bumping heads with the small black cat. Kitty wasn't the only human with the special ability to turn into a cat—her grandma could do it too! Kitty still found it incredible—and, of course, it meant she had another amazing thing in common with her grandmother.

Kitty and her grandma joined in as the cats gathered under a nearby tree, eagerly eyeing the small birds collecting in its branches. They meowed in disappointment as the birds suddenly scattered, flying up into the sky—but they were soon distracted by a game of chase with a couple of butterflies that

were fluttering past. The cats ran after them happily, swatting at them as they danced through the air. Kitty still wasn't sure why chasing after things was so much fun as a cat, but she definitely enjoyed it as much as the others did!

"Oh, look, there's Coco!" meowed Bella breathlessly, nodding toward a cat which was a short distance away. "And who's that kitten with her? I've never seen her before."

Kitty watched as Coco padded over to them to say hello. Coco was an elegant British Shorthair, with thick blue-gray fur, gleaming golden eyes, and a beautiful velvet collar. Coco could sometimes be a little bit snooty, but most of the time she was friendly with the other cats in town. Today, though, Kitty sensed she was in a bad mood.

"Hi, Coco," Bella said. "Who are you with?"

"Oh, that's Ruby," Coco meowed grumpily, nodding at the kitten eagerly trotting along behind her. "My humans adopted her last week."

Kitty smiled over at Ruby. "I met little Ruby at your house today, Coco," Kitty replied. "I know your humans— Evie's one of my school friends, and I was playing at her house this afternoon!" That was another one of the nice things about Kitty's special gift: she often knew both the humans and the cats in one family. Evie and her parents were Coco's owners. When they'd heard that a kitten needed a new home, they'd decided she would be good company for Coco. Kitty thought that Coco didn't seem very happy about it all, though. She curled her tail around her body primly and sighed.

"Yes, I was playing in the yard next door, but I could hear you all making a fuss over Ruby," Coco said, sounding a bit annoyed.

Just then, Ruby caught up with them and gave a bright, cheerful meow. "Hello, big cats!"

The other cats meowed in greeting too.

"Hi, Ruby!" Kitty replied with a friendly meow. "Nice to see you again!

I'm Kitty. We met earlier at your house."

The leopard-like kitten looked a bit confused. "Were you hiding at the end of the yard? That's where my friend Coco goes sometimes, and I have to go and find her!"

Coco flicked the tip of her tail and Kitty thought she saw her roll her eyes.

"No, I was one of the girls that was playing with you and your human, Evie! I have a special ability, you see—I can turn into a cat!"

Ruby ran around in a circle, her fur ruffling, and did a little bounce. "Wow! That's amazing! I've never heard of a human who could be a cat too!"

Kitty giggled and then noticed that Ruby's small paws were covered in mud.

"She's been playing in a dirty puddle," Coco told them, shuddering as Ruby trotted away, curious about a black beetle that was crawling past. Coco always took great care with her grooming, and she seemed irritated that two of the other cats were meowing to each other about the lovely pattern on the little kitten's coat, when Ruby didn't even care about how she looked.

"It must be nice to have a new young cat at home to play with," said Bella wistfully.

But Coco wrinkled her nose. "It's so annoying," she grumbled. "Ever since Ruby arrived, my humans have barely paid any attention to me. If they're not cooing over their new baby, they're playing with Ruby and taking pictures of her with their hand-screen things. They seem to think everything she does is funny and cute."

Just then, Ruby caught sight of the pond nearby. With an excited mew, she dashed over to it, pouncing playfully toward a duck that was snoozing in the sunshine at the water's edge. With a squawk of surprise, the duck flapped his wings and took off into the air, splashing water everywhere— including over Coco!

"Ugh! I hate getting wet!" snapped Coco, shaking the droplets of water out of her fur.

The other cats giggled as Ruby bounded around happily, enjoying all the new sights and smells of the park, but Kitty watched Coco bristle angrily.

I'd better keep an eye on Coco and Ruby, Kitty thought. *Coco can be a little bit mean*

*when things don't go her way. This could
lead to some trouble!*

The following evening, Kitty was reading
a book in the backyard when she caught
sight of a symbol scratched into a tree
trunk nearby: three small claw marks in
the shape of a triangle. Kitty knew
instantly what that symbol meant: one
of the neighborhood cats wanted to
call a meeting of the Cat Council. Local
cats scratched that symbol into posts and
trees whenever they needed to call a
meeting, and Kitty knew that she needed
to be there.

The Cat Council was a secret gather-
ing of all the cats in town. Its job was to
listen to any problems the cats had, and

to try to help solve them. Tiger, a rather bossy but kind tomcat, was the leader of the Cat Council, but Kitty had a very special role too. She was the Guardian, which meant it was up to her to give advice to any cat in need. The other cats particularly liked to ask for Kitty's advice whenever they had a problem that had something to do with humans. Of course, Kitty under-stood the human world in a way all the ordinary cats couldn't! Grandma had been the Guardian before Kitty, and Kitty was very proud to have taken over, even though she still had things to learn.

A couple of hours later, Kitty was waiting impatiently for dinner to be over so that she could make up an excuse to go to bed early. When she was finally allowed to leave the table, Kitty helped Grandma clean up and whispered to her about the symbol she'd seen in the yard.

"We'd better both go there as soon as we can, Kitty!" replied Grandma.

After pretending to go to bed early, Kitty and Grandma transformed into their cat forms and slipped through the open kitchen window. Kitty loved padding through the town on a spring evening. The air was always full of interesting smells, and Kitty's cat nose was very sensitive. She could smell flowers and herbs from the yards and, of course, the scents of every single

cat in town. Each cat had a different scent, and Kitty was getting to know them all, one by one.

She followed Grandma up the street, leaped nimbly over a fence, ran along a wall, and finally made her way through an alleyway to the woods. The Cat

Council always met in the same clearing, and up ahead Kitty could see that a circle of cats had already started to gather. There were cats of every different kind in the Council, from tough old tomcats to elegant purebreds with pedigrees.

Kitty bumped heads with all her friends, including a quiet black cat named Shadow and a shy little kitten called Petal. She took her place in between Tiger and Grandma. When the last cats had arrived, Tiger started the meeting.

"Good evening, everyone! Settle down, please! Let's begin by saying the Meow Vow," he told them.

Together, all the cats in the circle recited the words that they said at the start of every Cat Council meeting:

"When you meow,
  We promise now,
  This solemn vow,
  To help somehow."

"Excellent!" said Tiger. "Now, which cat called this meeting? Please step forward and tell us how we can help."

To her surprise, Kitty saw Coco step primly onto a tree stump in the middle of the circle. Coco always attended the Cat Council meetings, but she had never called one herself before. Kitty glanced around to see where Ruby, the little kitten who now shared Coco's house, was sitting. There were a couple of other small cats around the circle, but Ruby wasn't one of them . . .

Suddenly, Kitty thought she could

guess what Coco was about to ask the Cat Council for help with. She just hoped she was wrong.

"*I* called this meeting, Tiger," Coco announced, swishing her fluffy tail. "I have something very important to discuss. It's about the kitten my humans have just adopted—Ruby."

"And is Ruby here today?" asked Tiger, glancing around.

Coco shook her head. "She's too little to know about the Cat Council, and I'm afraid I made sure not to tell her about the meeting," she explained.

"Oh. I hope nothing too serious has happened. Do tell us what the problem is," meowed Tiger, looking concerned.

Coco paused dramatically, looking around the circle. "I've decided that enough is enough," she declared. "It's just not fair, and I don't want that little fluff ball around any more. Ruby *has* to go!"

Chapter 3

All around the circle, the cats gasped.

Tiger shook his ginger head, looking very worried. "The Cat Council wants all cats to feel welcome in our town," he explained. "We would never want to force any cat to leave!"

There was a chorus of agreement from around the circle.

"I don't mind if Ruby stays in town,"

Coco told Tiger sulkily, "but I don't want her to live in my house any more."

"Why do you feel this way, Coco?" asked Grandma gently.

"Yes—Ruby's so pretty, and she seems so playful and fun!" added Misty.

Coco scowled. "That's just the problem!" she huffed. "She never sits still! She tries to play-fight with me all the time, and messes up my lovely fur. She treads muddy paw prints through the kitchen. She drinks my milk, and she's even started taking cat naps in my special place underneath the radiator! But worst of all, my humans think everything she does is adorable. They don't pay any attention to me any more, even though they've been my family for years and years. Now Ruby's come along and ruined everything! It's just not fair. I want another family to adopt Ruby instead, so that things can go back to the way they were before."

There were mutters of disapproval from around the circle. "Coco, you're just being selfish," meowed a Persian cat named Emerald.

Kitty agreed—but then she felt Grandma nudging her with a paw. "Kitty, as our Guardian, you must try to find a way to help Coco, as hard as that may be," she whispered.

Kitty hesitated. How could she help Coco? This felt like the hardest problem

she'd ever been faced with. She knew
Grandma was right, though. She had to
do her best. She took a step forward,
and all the other cats hushed.

"Ah, Kitty! Perhaps our Guardian
can think of an answer," said Tiger,
sounding relieved.

"I hope so," answered Kitty. "Coco, I agree that Ruby seems like a bit of a handful at the moment, but don't you think that's just because she's so young? She's only a baby, really, and she's getting used to her new home. Over time, I think you might grow to like her. You might even find out that you have something in common."

"Kitty's right!" meowed Bella, and next to her, Misty nodded.

But Coco didn't look very impressed. "That advice is no help whatsoever," she told Kitty snootily. "I don't *want* to wait around for Ruby to grow up. I need things to change right now!"

Kitty didn't know what to say. Since she'd become the Guardian, she'd always been able to come up with a solution for every problem—until this one! "Er . . . I'll think of another way to help, I promise," she told the irritated cat.

"Hmm. I don't think so," huffed Coco, turning her back on Kitty, stepping down from the tree stump and slinking away.

"Maybe you have lots of human knowledge, Kitty, but you don't know enough about cats to help me out. This was a waste of time! I'm going home."

As Coco disappeared from the clearing, Kitty took a deep, shaky breath. The circle of cats began meowing and muttering anxiously, although Tiger tried to call for quiet. Grandma rubbed her head against Kitty's reassuringly, and Misty trotted up to her friend to give her a friendly head bump. "Don't listen to Coco, Kitty," Misty told her earnestly. "You're a great Guardian! Everyone says so."

"And you *will* find a way to help Coco," Grandma told Kitty. "I know you will!"

Chapter 4

"Kitty, that was an awesome goal!" said Jenny as the girls walked out of soccer practice together the next day.

"Thanks!" replied Kitty, smiling. "You scored three! And you were great too, Evie," she added, catching sight of their friend walking over to join them.

Evie grinned at them. "I've been practicing my shots in the backyard," she explained. "Whenever I haven't been playing with Ruby, that is. She's just so sweet, I get distracted!"

Evie only talks about Ruby these days— never Coco, Kitty thought, as Evie chatted about her little kitten. Kitty felt a pang of sympathy for the grumpy pedigree cat.

"It's funny to think that you have two babies in your house at the moment," commented Jenny, smiling. "One cat baby and one human baby—Ruby and Joe!"

Kitty realized Jenny was right. Ruby was just like Joe: a new baby in the family! And maybe Evie and Coco were both feeling the same way: annoyed that the babies of the family were getting all the attention. Kitty decided to ask Evie if she was getting used to having Joe around now. As an only child, Kitty didn't know how it felt to have a new sibling, but Evie had been a big sister for three months. *She might have some tips or ideas that could help with Coco's problem*, Kitty thought.

"Jenny's right. You're really lucky, Evie!" she said. "Do you like being a big sister?"

Evie hesitated. "Sometimes," she admitted. "When Joe's being quiet and smiling, or he's giggling, then he's really cute. He's annoying when he cries, though—Mom and Dad just stop talking to me or listening to me and go straight to him. Once Mom was so

busy looking after Joe, she forgot to get my dinner out of the oven, and it burned! I think that's why they got Ruby for me," she added, "so that I wouldn't feel left out."

Kitty nodded, but nothing Evie had said had given her any ideas about how to help Coco.

All the way home, Kitty thought about Coco's problem. Finally, as she sat down for dinner with Grandma and her parents, she decided what to do. *I'll pay Coco a surprise visit tonight,* she thought. *Talking to Evie didn't help, but talking to Coco again might.*

That night, as soon as she heard her parents' bedroom door close, Kitty crept downstairs and into the moonlit yard. Very quietly, she whispered the words on her silver pendant and transformed into her cat form.

Kitty scrambled up onto the roof of her playhouse and from there leaped onto the top of the back fence. Using her tail, her whiskers, and her strong, sharp claws for balance, she ran nimbly along the fence, through her neighbors' yards, past the park, and then down the next street. Evie lived in a little cottage just past the post office.

Kitty darted into the backyard. Evie's toys were scattered all over the grass, and Kitty saw a clothesline full of tiny baby clothes swinging gently in the breeze. Now that she was here, she was a bit nervous. Coco hadn't exactly been friendly the last time Kitty had seen her. Still, she took a deep breath and was about to nudge the cat flap open with her head when she heard a curious meow behind her.

"Kitty? Is that you?"

Kitty whirled around, her fur standing on end in surprise. Coco was curled up on Evie's trampoline, her golden eyes gleaming in the darkness.

"You made me jump, Coco!" Kitty meowed. "What are you doing?"

Coco looked very sulky. "Trying to get some sleep," she answered. "I used to sleep on Evie's lovely, cozy bed before that stupid fluff ball arrived. Now Ruby sleeps there instead. I know you think

I'm just being selfish, but how would *you* like it if that happened to you?"

Kitty nodded. "It does sound diffi-cult, Coco," she admitted. "I really want to find a way to help you. That's why I'm here!"

"Come inside," Coco told her, jumping down from the trampoline and trotting daintily over to the cat flap. "Then you'll see for yourself."

Kitty followed Coco through the cat flap and into the darkened kitchen. This was the first time she'd ever been in Evie's house in her cat form, and it felt really strange! Kitty stared around, her sharp cat eyes and ears picking up details she'd never noticed before, like the pattern of tiny dots on the tablecloth

and the whispery rustle of the plants on the window sill.

"Look!" said Coco, swishing her thick furry tail.

Kitty looked at where Coco's tail was pointing and saw an elegant china bowl on the kitchen floor, with *Coco* written on the side in swirly letters. Chunks of cat food were splattered all around it. "That's *my* special bowl, and Ruby thinks she can just help herself without asking," Coco explained. "She makes such a mess!"

"She *is* just a kitten," Kitty replied hesitantly. "I bet all kittens are messy eaters, Coco."

Coco snorted. "Not me! I was always a very delicate eater," she told Kitty. "And look up there, on the fridge."

Kitty glanced up and saw a series of photographs stuck to the fridge with magnets. Most of them were of Evie and Joe, but there were also three pictures of Ruby. In one of them, she was cuddled sweetly on Evie's lap. In the second, she was reaching a tiny paw up to touch a butterfly. In the third, she was chasing after a bouncy ball, with Evie giggling in the background. Kitty quickly scanned the rest of the pictures, but none were of Coco.

"See? She's taken over everything," Coco said angrily.

Kitty felt awful. She really could understand why Coco was so upset about Ruby. But she still couldn't see a way to help. "Where is Ruby now, Coco? Maybe we could try talking to her about this," she suggested.

"Probably curled up on Evie's bed—like I said, she sleeps there now," said Coco, padding into the hallway and up the stairs.

Kitty trotted after Coco, who nudged open the door to Evie's bedroom with her paw and nose. Peering inside, Kitty saw Evie snuggled under her star-patterned duvet—and curled up at the end of the bed was a tiny, fluffy heap.

"See? That's where *I* used to sleep," muttered Coco.

The spotted golden heap stirred, and Ruby lifted her head and blinked sleepily. "Coco?" she meowed. "And . . . Kitty! Have you come to play?" Suddenly, the little kitten was wide awake!

Kitty couldn't help giggling as Ruby sprang down from the bed excitedly and ran forward to bump heads with her. Coco narrowed her eyes, annoyed.

"What should we do? Should we play a game? We have lots of toys, don't we, Coco?" said Ruby eagerly.

"They're my toys, actually," Coco replied coldly. "And you're too little to play with us anyway, Ruby."

The kitten looked hurt, and Kitty felt sorry for Ruby. But before she could say anything, there was a wail from down the corridor. Kitty felt her ears prick up and saw Coco's and Ruby's do the same. Baby Joe had woken up, and he was crying—very noisily!

"Quick!" whispered Kitty urgently. "If Evie wakes up, she'll see me in her bedroom, and I'm not supposed to be here! I need to get downstairs, fast."

"Let's go!" agreed Coco, darting out of the bedroom and into the corridor. Kitty followed her, and she heard the tiny pad of Ruby's paws behind her as well.

"What an unhappy sound that is!" Kitty heard Evie's dad saying gently. "Come on now, shhh."

"Dad?"

Kitty froze at the top of the staircase, and her ears pricked up again as she heard Evie call out sleepily.

"Oh dear," said Dad, "it sounds like your big sister's awake now too."

"I'm just going downstairs to get a drink," said Evie.

"Okay, love. Back to bed straight after that," Evie's dad called back.

Kitty and the others darted down the stairs, but she heard the thump of Evie's footsteps coming soon after. There wasn't time to run for the cat flap. Evie would be in the kitchen at any moment!

Chapter 5

Kitty turned to Coco. "Where should I hide? I can't let Evie see me!" she whispered anxiously.

"Over there, behind the recycling bin," suggested Coco. "Quickly!"

Kitty dashed into the kitchen and crouched behind the big green recycling bin. She tucked her white-tipped tail in and flattened her ears so that nothing was poking out. Just as she did, the kitchen door opened wider and the light came on. Kitty heard Evie step into the kitchen.

"Ruby! What are you doing down here? You were cuddled up on my bed when I went to sleep," Evie cooed down at the little kitten.

Kitty peered carefully around the recycling bin and saw her friend bend down and gently scoop Ruby up.

Evie stroked the fur between the kitten's ears, while Ruby purred happily. "Maybe you're hungry," Evie suggested. "How about a little snack?"

Kitty watched as Coco rubbed against Evie's ankles, meowing hopefully. To her surprise, Evie didn't even glance

down at Coco. She was paying too much attention to Ruby to even notice her older cat. *Evie's not behaving very fairly*, Kitty thought to herself. *Poor Coco.*

Evie put Ruby down and rummaged in a cupboard. She pulled out a box and scattered a handful of kitten treats in a little saucer, placing it on the floor next to Ruby. As Ruby dug in happily, Evie went over to the sink and ran herself a glass of water. She called, "Night night, Ruby!" then headed back upstairs, switching the light off as she went.

Kitty waited for a moment or two while her cat eyes adjusted to the dark again. When she was sure the coast was clear, she stepped out from her hiding place. She had decided she would talk to Evie at school tomorrow and try to put in a good word for Coco. If Evie gave *both* cats lots of love and attention, Coco wouldn't feel so left out.

But as she was about to explain her plan, Coco let out a nasty growl.

"It's not fair!" the gray cat snapped,

reaching out a fluffy paw and knocking Ruby's dish of kitten treats over. As the food scattered over the floor, she turned to the tiny kitten so that they were whisker to whisker. Angrily she hissed, "I wish you'd just go away, Ruby. And never come back!" And with that, she stormed across the kitchen and out of the cat flap.

Ruby was wide-eyed as the cat-flap door swung closed again. Kitty understood why Ruby was a bit taken aback. Coco could be quite scary when she was angry.

"Why is Coco being so mean?" Ruby asked, sounding confused. "What did I do?"

"Oh dear. Don't worry, Ruby. Coco's just a bit upset right now. Everything will be okay," she reassured the kitten. "I'm going to find a way for you and Coco to get along, I promise!"

Kitty walked into school the next morning feeling very determined. She wasn't sure how to help Ruby and Coco in her cat form, but at least there was one thing she could do as a human. *I'm going to find Evie as soon as I arrive,* she told herself. *I'm going to talk to her about Coco, and tell her that she needs to pay attention to* both *cats!*

But when Kitty spotted Evie in the playground, she immediately knew that something was wrong. Evie's face was pink and blotchy, as if she had been crying, and Jenny had a comforting arm around their friend.

"What happened, Evie?" Kitty asked, rushing over to her. "Is everything okay?"

"It's my kitten, Ruby!" Evie said with a sniff, her eyes filling with tears. "She's gone missing!"

Chapter 6

"What? What do you mean, gone missing?" asked Kitty, shocked.

"Ruby wasn't in the house or the yard this morning," Evie sobbed. "She sometimes goes exploring, but she's always back at breakfast time. She's never missed it before, not once. Mom and Dad helped me look for her before school, but we couldn't find her anywhere. I'm so worried something awful has happened to her!"

"I'm sure she'll be okay, Evie," said Kitty, hugging her friend. "I bet by the time school finishes today, she'll have turned up. And if she hasn't, we'll help you look for her."

Poor Evie was upset and anxious all day and couldn't concentrate on her schoolwork. When it was time to go home, Kitty's class ran outside to the school gates. Evie's dad was there to pick Evie up, and Kitty could see from the worried look on his face that Ruby hadn't been found yet.

Grandma was picking up Kitty and Jenny today, and Kitty quickly explained what had happened.

"We'll have a good look on our way home, girls," agreed Grandma, looking very serious. "That poor little kitten . . ."

Kitty, Jenny, and Grandma walked home very slowly. Grandma glanced over hedges, and Kitty paused to check underneath every parked car they passed. They all called Ruby's name loudly, and Jenny even peeped inside one or two garbage cans, just in case Ruby had somehow fallen inside. But by the time they reached their street, there had been no sign of her.

Suddenly, Kitty had an idea. The other *cats* in town might be able to help search for Ruby! They were much more likely to know places a cat might hide. Kitty waited until Jenny had stepped inside her house and closed the front

door. She quickly glanced around to make sure that no one else was nearby except Grandma. "I think we'd better change into our cat forms, Grandma. I have to call a Cat Council meeting right away!"

Grandma nodded. "I think you're right, Kitty," she said, looking worried. Together, they hid behind a tall rosebush in the yard and, a few moments later, trotted out on their paws. But just as Kitty was about to scratch the special triangular symbol into a nearby telephone post, she saw Misty dart out of her front yard, her big blue eyes wide.

"Oh, Kitty, Suki, thank goodness," the silver tabby panted. "An emergency Cat Council meeting has just been called!"

Kitty and her grandma exchanged glances. Who could have called the meeting already?

Together, Kitty, Misty, and Grandma raced toward the woods, their tails streaking out behind them. As they padded into the clearing, Kitty was surprised to see more cats gathered there than she had ever seen before. It seemed like not only were all the cats from town there, but all the cats from the neighboring towns too!

"When I found out that a little kitten had gone missing, I just had to come along and help," Kitty heard Pinky, an unusual cat with no fur, explain.

"So did I!" agreed Sooty, a fluffy white cat with patches of black fur. "I hope we find her. The poor little thing must be so frightened."

"I bet her humans are worried sick!" added Shadow, the older, sleek black cat who Kitty had helped not too long ago.

Kitty ran over to sit beside Misty and Tiger. "Who called the meeting?" she asked breathlessly, still puzzled. *Who else knew that Ruby was missing?*

"Yes, who called this emergency meeting?" asked Tiger, addressing the whole group. "Please step forward."

Kitty gasped as *Coco* padded into the circle! Instead of acting sulky and cross, the elegant cat looked worried and frightened. Her whiskers drooped and her fur, usually so groomed and tidy, was sticking up messily.

"*I* called the meeting," she announced, her voice shaky. "I live with Ruby, the little kitten who's gone missing. I . . . I think it was all my fault!"

"Oh dear. Tell us what happened, Coco," Tiger encouraged her kindly.

"I was so nasty to her," Coco admitted. "I told her to go away. Then, by this morning, she had disappeared! I think she ran off because of what I said. I didn't really mean it, though. I just wish she'd come home safe and sound!"

"We'll find her, Coco," Kitty said.

"I should have listened to your advice, Kitty!" meowed Coco miserably. "I should have tried to get along with Ruby, instead of only thinking of myself. I feel terrible. I've been looking for her everywhere—in the yard, in our garage, even in the horrid cobwebby shed. That's why my fur's such a mess!"

"She can't have gone very far," Kitty reassured her. "I think we should all split up. That way, we'll be able to search more places. If we all get into teams of two, hopefully we'll find Ruby in no time."

"Good idea, Kitty!" agreed Tiger. "Let's see. Misty and Bruno, you take the playground. Petal and Emerald, you look around the park. Smoky and Shadow, check the alleyways . . ."

Tiger gave all the cats a different area to search. Kitty decided to go with Coco.

"Why don't we go back to your street, Coco?" Kitty suggested. "I'm sure Ruby won't have gone very far. Perhaps she's somewhere close to home."

"Check all the yards and under all the cars," Tiger called to the cats as they headed off. "Remember to look in playhouses and underneath trampolines too!"

"Come on, Coco!" said Kitty. "Let's go!"

The two cats raced back to Coco's street. As they ran toward Coco's house, Kitty saw Evie's dad sticking up a flyer to a lamp-post. It showed a picture of Ruby, with the word *LOST* scribbled above it in Evie's handwriting, and a phone number below. Evie's dad was holding a thick stack of the flyers, and Kitty guessed he was planning to stick them up all over town.

"Where shall we look first, Coco?"

Kitty asked, as Evie's dad walked further away down the street. "Any ideas? Where do you think Ruby might hide?"

Coco shook her head anxiously. "I don't know," she admitted. "I don't even know what Ruby likes, or where her favorite places are."

"Well, where would *you* go?" asked Kitty. "Imagine you're feeling sad, or grumpy, or you just want to be by yourself."

Coco paused, thinking hard. Then she looked at Kitty, her golden eyes wide. "That's it! I've thought of somewhere!" she said excitedly. "Thank you, Kitty! How could I not have thought of this before now? Follow me!"

Chapter 7

"Wait, Coco! Why are we going back inside your house?" said Kitty, puzzled as she followed Coco.

"That's just it! I think that's where Ruby might be," explained Coco.

Eagerly she leaped through the cat flap and ran up the stairs. Kitty followed, wondering if Coco was heading toward Evie's bedroom—but she was surprised to see Coco dart into baby Joe's room instead. Kitty trotted after her on her quick paws, feeling even more confused.

"You think Ruby's in here?" she asked Coco.

Next to Joe's empty cot was a comfy-looking rocking chair with a blanket spread over it. Next to that was a chest of drawers, painted white with a pattern of little bunnies. A wooden toy box was sitting on top of the chest of drawers. It was packed with stuffed animals, their fluffy ears poking out. But there was no sign of the little kitten.

Coco nodded at the toy box. "There!" she told Kitty. "Sometimes, when I'm feeling really bad, I go and sit in that

toy box. It's cozy and warm and quiet in there. Ruby might have seen me do it before and decided to hide there herself!"

Coco sprang onto the rocking chair, making it rock backward and forward. Taking a second to get her balance, she then jumped up onto the chest of drawers. Kitty did the same, landing with a gentle thud beside the gray cat. She peered inside the toy box with Coco, and they used their paws to push the teddy bears and soft toys aside. Suddenly there was a tiny squeak of surprise from inside the box, and something moved.

"I was right!" meowed Coco happily.

"Ruby!" cried Kitty.

A tiny spotted head slowly peeped

out from among the toys, and a pair of big eyes blinked nervously.

When Ruby saw Coco, she gave a yelp of worry and scrabbled to jump out of the box, as if she was about to run away again. Kitty gasped as the toy box wobbled with the sudden movement. "Ruby, don't move! The toy box

is right on the edge of the chest of drawers. If you jump out, I think it might topple off!" she warned.

"I'm sorry I was so mean to you, Ruby!" meowed Coco. "Please don't run off again. I promise I'm going to be nicer to you from now on."

But the little kitten was still upset and wasn't listening. With a meow, she leaped from the toy box down to the carpet. As she did, the whole box wobbled forward and tumbled down after her, with toys and teddy bears spilling out everywhere! The box landed upside down—with Ruby trapped underneath it!

"Ruby!" meowed Coco anxiously, jumping down quickly from the chest of drawers and pushing at the box with her paws. "Kitty, help! It's too heavy to move by myself."

Kitty jumped down too, but even when both cats tried nudging the box together, it didn't move. "Ruby, are you okay under there?" Kitty meowed to her worriedly.

"I think so," Ruby squeaked, her voice sounding muffled from under the box. "I'm not hurt. But it's very dark in here. I want to get out!"

Kitty's mind was racing. As a cat, she couldn't help Ruby, but if she turned back into her human form, she'd be able to lift the box easily! It would be very risky, though. If Evie or one of her parents found her there, her magical secret would be lost forever . . .

But Kitty didn't have time to make her mind up—there were footsteps in the corridor outside, and Evie's voice called, "Mom, is that you? I just heard a funny noise in Joe's room."

Kitty had to hide again! Quickly, she

squeezed underneath Joe's cot. Peeping out from underneath, she saw a pair of spotty yellow socks appear in the doorway.

"Coco!" Evie said, sounding very surprised. "What are you doing in here? Oh, you naughty cat! You've knocked over the toy box!"

No, she's not being naughty! Look underneath it! thought Kitty, silently pleading with Evie. *Look underneath the box!*

Coco was trying her best to show Evie what had happened. Meowing loudly, she patted the box with her paws and nudged it with her head.

"What are you doing, Coco? I don't have time to play with you. I've got to find Ruby," scolded Evie.

Hearing her name, Ruby let out a few squeaky little meows from underneath the box. Kitty held her breath.

"Ruby!" Evie cried. Kneeling quickly, she lifted the box. Ruby scampered out and pounced toward Evie's legs, rubbing against them and meowing excitedly. "You were here all along!" Evie said. "And it was Coco who found you. Clever, clever Coco!"

She bent down and picked up Coco, giving her a long cuddle. Coco purred happily, rubbing the top of her head against Evie's chin. Hidden under the cot, Kitty had to try very hard not to start purring herself, in case Evie heard the noise.

Ruby's been found safe and sound, and Evie knows that it's all because of Coco, she thought, watching Evie plant kisses all over Coco's head. *Maybe now she'll pay Coco more attention, and Coco and Ruby will get along better!*

"Kitty! Jenny! Guess what?" Evie called, running into the playground the next morning. "Ruby's okay!"

"Hooray!" cried Jenny. "Where was she?"

"She didn't run away. She was in our house all along!" explained Evie, laughing. "She'd been hiding in Joe's toy box. Mom and Dad couldn't believe it. We didn't even find her ourselves—it was Coco!"

"Wow! What a clever cat," said Kitty, with a secret smile to herself. "You must be really happy, Evie."

"Yes. I'm so relieved!" Evie agreed. "We've been totally spoiling *both* cats ever since we found little Ruby. Mom bought some special fancy cat food as a treat, and a new collar for each of them. Dad even said that both of them could sleep on my bed. I wasn't sure they would do it, because they'd never slept there together before, but they curled up in a furry ball side by side, purring! It was *so* cute!"

"You're so lucky, Evie," Jenny said as the three girls walked into their classroom, "having *two* gorgeous cats to play with!"

"I know! *And* a baby brother," said Evie happily. "When Ruby ran away, it made me realize how sad I'd be if anything bad happened to Joe. He's only little, just like her—I should be helping to look after him, not getting annoyed by him!"

Kitty grinned. It looked like helping Coco and Ruby had solved Evie's problem too!

That night, Kitty changed into her cat form once her parents had gone to bed. She leaped off her window, landing sure and steady on her four paws, and made her way straight over to Evie's street, hoping to find Coco and Ruby. She came across both cats playing in their backyard together.

"Hi, Kitty!" meowed Ruby cheer-fully. "Coco's teaching me how to call a Cat Council meeting, in case I ever have to do it myself."

"That's great, Ruby," Kitty told the little kitten. "It must be lovely having an older cat like Coco to learn things from."

"Thank you, Kitty. You really helped me to see that I shouldn't just think about myself. I wasn't very nice to Ruby at first," Coco admitted sheepishly. "But I'm going to look after her from now on."

"It's so much fun doing things together!" Ruby purred, looking happily at Coco. "Guess what, Kitty? We've even tried cuddling up under the radiator together, and we both fit!"

"In fact, it's even cozier with two!" added Coco, chuckling.

Kitty giggled, delighted to see her friends getting along so well. She was happy too because, as Guardian, she had been able to help them out. Even

though this had been her trickiest chal-
lenge yet, she was already looking
forward to her next cat adventure!

MEET

Kitty

Kitty is a little girl who can magically turn into a cat! She is the Guardian of the Cat Council.

Tiger

Tiger is a big, brave tabby tomcat. He is leader of the Cat Council.

Suki

Suki is Kitty's grandmother. She can magically turn into a cat too!

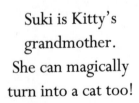

THE CATS

Ruby

Ruby is a kitten who always wants to play. Ruby is a Bengal kitten— which means she looks like a tiny leopard!

Coco is a very glamorous cat. She just loves to be the center of attention.

Coco

Smoky

Smoky is a plump, friendly female cat. Her fur is very fluffy and all her paws are white.

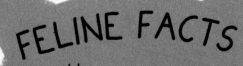

FELINE FACTS

Here are some
fun facts about our
purrrfect animal friends
that you might like
to know...

1.

Cats hide when
they are **jealous**.

2.

Cats can't see directly
below their **noses**.

3.

A cat can jump up to **seven times** its height!

4.

A group of kittens is called a **"kindle"** and a group of cats is called a **"clowder."**

5.

Cats can be **right-** or **left-pawed,** the same way people are right- or left-handed!

Kitty visits her family on a farm and
meets Star, the farm cat!

Can Kitty help Star
befriend a new puppy?

Read on for a glimpse of
Kitty's next adventure . . .

"Just one more sleep until my trip!" said Kitty Kimura. "I hope I like Aunt Wendy's farm."

Kitty's grandma looked at her. "I can tell you're a little bit nervous, Kitty," she said gently. "But I'm sure you'll love it at Strawberry Lane Farm. It's just beautiful!"

It was the start of the summer

vacation, and Kitty was helping her grandma at the family's shop on Willow Street. Kitty's parents were on a trip to Japan, where her dad and her grandma came from. They were buying lots of supplies for the shop, which sold special Japanese things.

Kitty missed them, but it was fun spending time with Grandma. Tomorrow, though, she was leaving for Strawberry Lane Farm, where Aunt Wendy and Uncle Greg lived. A real farm! Kitty's mom had told her it had lots of cows and horses, coops full of chickens, and a huge meadow dotted with strawberries, which gave the farm its pretty name. It was several hours away by train, and Kitty had never been there before. She'd never been away on her own before, either.

"You'll only be away for two nights, and Aunt Wendy and Uncle Greg will take very good care of you," Grandma went on. "Your cousin Max will be there too. I bet you'll be best friends right away. You're going to have a lovely time."

Kitty nodded, but she still felt a little bit uncertain. She *was* looking forward to seeing Strawberry Lane Farm, and to seeing Max again—but it all felt so far away from home, from Grandma, and from her best friend, Jenny, who Kitty usually saw every single day of the summer holidays.

Grandma smiled at Kitty, her eyes

twinkling. "I know what will cheer you up," she said. "Strawberry Lane Farm has lots of animals—including a cat!"

"Really?" Kitty's eyes lit up, and she grinned at Grandma. "I've never met a farm cat before. I think I *will* like Strawberry Lane Farm!"

Once they'd closed the shop that evening, Kitty asked Grandma if she could go out for a while.

"Of course, Kitty," Grandma replied. "I know you have a special friend to say goodbye to! Don't stay out too late, though. Remember, you've got a long journey tomorrow."

Kitty grinned. She'd already said goodbye to Jenny earlier that day.

Grandma was talking about another friend—a four-legged one. She gave Grandma a kiss on the cheek, then raced into the backyard. She glanced around quickly, to make sure that none of the neighbors was in sight. Then she reached for the silver pendant hanging around her neck, which had a picture of a cat engraved on it. Quietly, she recited the magic words.

"Human hands to kitten paws,
  Human fingers, kitten claws."

Kitty closed her eyes and waited. Suddenly, a fizzing feeling swept through her toes, then into her feet and up her legs. Kitty grinned as the bubbling, tickling sensation whooshed through her whole body. No matter how many times it happened, Kitty never quite got used to how strange it felt!

When the feeling faded away, Kitty opened her eyes and looked around. Suddenly, the oak tree and the play-house at the end of the yard looked ten times bigger. Although it was twilight

and the yard was dim, Kitty could see every blade of grass and every flower petal vividly. Her nose filled with the beautiful scent of Grandma's lavender and rosebushes, and her ears picked up the faintest noises from the other side of the yard: the buzzing of a bee and the chattering of a line of tiny ants. Kitty's senses were more powerful for a magical reason—she had turned into a small black cat!

Being able to turn into a cat was Kitty's big secret. The only other person who knew was Grandma—because she had the same special ability too. It was Grandma who had given Kitty her necklace and taught her the magic words. Grandma had also introduced Kitty to the Cat Council, which was a nighttime meeting of all the cats in the neighborhood. Kitty even had a special role in the Cat Council: she was the Guardian. This meant cats could come to her with problems or questions, and she would try to help them.

Kitty loved her secret life as a cat, although it had taken her a while to get used to having a tail! Her favorite thing to do in cat form was explore the town late at night—while all her human family and friends were fast asleep—with her new cat friends for company.

Kitty stretched her furry black legs and flexed her paws, then leaped onto the backyard fence and trotted along it. As she walked, her tail swayed from side to side, helping her to balance. She was heading for her best friend Jenny's house—where her best cat friend also lived.

"Hi, Misty!" Kitty meowed, jumping down into the backyard, where a small

silver tabby was curled up on Jenny's trampoline.

Misty sprang up when she saw Kitty, her blue eyes gleaming. The two cats bumped foreheads to say hello.

"Kitty! I'm so glad you came to see me. I thought you might have already left for your aunt's farm!" purred Misty.

"I wouldn't leave without saying goodbye, Misty. I'm leaving tomorrow," Kitty explained. "Grandma's taking me on the train after lunch. And guess what? There's a cat at the farm!"

"A farm cat! I've never met one of those before," Misty meowed excitedly. "I've never even been to a farm," she added. "I've only ever lived in a town. I wonder what it will be like."

Kitty purred thoughtfully. "I think it's going to be very big, with lots of grass and places to run around," she said. "Mom says Aunt Wendy and Uncle Greg have some black-and-white cows, some chickens, and a huge, scary-looking bull. I'm going to stay away from him! And I think there'll be lots of trees to climb."

"Climbing trees is my favorite. I wish I was going with you!" said Misty wistfully. "We'd have so much fun there together. But at least you'll have the farm cat to play with."

"I wish you were coming too! I'll tell you all about it as soon as I get back. I just hope the farm cat is friendly," said Kitty, a little anxiously.

Most of the cats she'd met since discovering her secret gift had been very nice, but not all. Just like people, Kitty had found that cats had very different personalities!

The next day, Grandma and Kitty caught a train into the city, then another, smaller train into the countryside where Aunt Wendy and Uncle Greg lived. Kitty watched out the window as the tall buildings and busy traffic turned into wide open fields dotted with sheep and cows and the occasional scarecrow. She smiled at Grandma, but her tummy felt as though it were full of butterflies.

Finally, the train pulled into a little station. "Kitty, this is our stop!" said Grandma, reaching for Kitty's suitcase. The butterflies in Kitty's tummy fluttered even more.

As Kitty and Grandma stepped off the train, Kitty heard a friendly voice calling her name. "Kitty, over here!"

Aunt Wendy came running toward them, waving. She looked just like Kitty's mom, with the same wavy blond hair and freckles. She was dressed in a T-shirt, jeans, and sturdy green rubber boots that were blotchy with mud. Kitty hoped she'd packed the right sort of clothes for a farm. She hadn't really been sure what to bring.

"It's so good to see you both!" said Aunt Wendy, hugging Kitty and Grandma. "Kitty, you remember Max, don't you? You two are about the same age, although it's been a while since you've seen one another."

Kitty turned and saw her cousin, who was standing a little awkwardly nearby, his hands stuffed into his pockets. He had messy sandy-brown hair that fell into his eyes. Kitty smiled and said, "Hi, Max."

Max just nodded and looked away. "Can we go home now, Mom?" he muttered.

"Maybe he's shy, Kitty. Don't worry, he'll warm up to you," Grandma whispered, as they followed Aunt Wendy and Max to the car.

Ella Moonheart grew up telling fun and exciting stories to anyone who would listen. Now that she's an author, she's thrilled to be able to tell stories to so many more children with her Kitty's Magic books. Ella loves animals, but cats most of all! She wishes she could turn into one just like Kitty, but she's happy to just play with her pet cat, Nibbles—when she's not writing her books, of course!